Robins in their nest.

Tossing, turning veggies

need to get some rest.

Turnips tucked in tightly.

Potatoes closing eyes.

Tired out tomatoes

humming lullabies.

Cuddly cauliflowers.

Droopy pods of peas.

Rhubarb reading stories
to worn-out broccoli.

Baby carrots snuggling.
Baby lettuce too.

Aubergines are dreaming...

of places far and new.

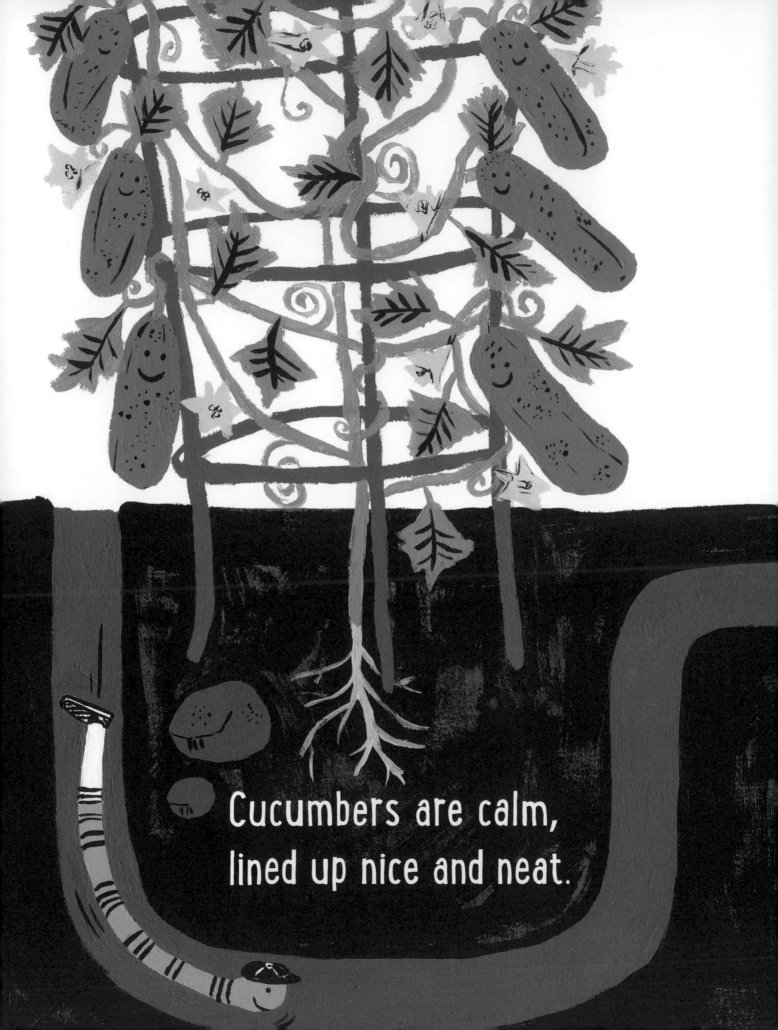

Cucumbers are calm,
lined up nice and neat.

Sweet potatoes rest.

Beetroots are simply beat.

Cabbages are nodding
their leafy, sleepy heads.

Radishes are dozing
in cosy garden beds.

Celery is snoring
as sunset disappears.

Cranky corn rolls over
and covers up its ears.

Every veggie's snoozing,

beneath the moon so bright,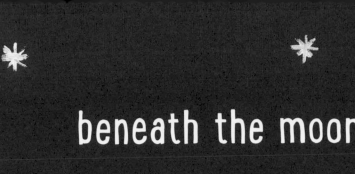

for nothing's more exhausting

than growing day and night.

Goodnight, sleepy veggies!
Sleep tight!

For my parents, who taught me to love veggies – D.M.

For Lydia, who has never met a veggie she couldn't stick in vinegar – Z.O.

More books to enjoy:

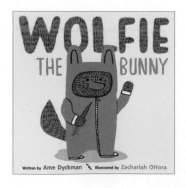 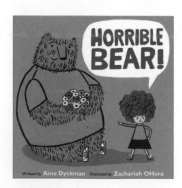 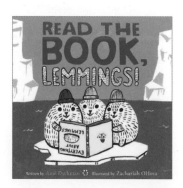

First published in Great Britain in 2021 by Andersen Press Ltd..

20 Vauxhall Bridge Road. London SW1V 2SA.

Published by special arrangement with Houghton Mifflin Harcourt Publishing Company. and Rights People. London.

Text copyright © 2020 by Diana Murray

Illustrations copyright © 2020 by Zachariah OHora

The rights of Diana Murray and Zachariah OHora to be identified as the author and

illustrator of this work have been asserted by them in accordance

with the Copyright. Designs and Patents Act. 1988.

All rights reserved.

Printed and bound in China.

1 3 5 7 9 10 8 6 4 2

British Library Cataloguing in Publication Data available.

ISBN 978 1 83913 043 4